The Burning Artist

Also by Mario Milosevic

Novels
Claypot Dreamstance
The Coma Monologues
The Doctor and the Clown
Kyle's War
The Last Giant
Splitting
Terrastina and Mazolli

Collections
15 Strange Tales of Crime and Mystery
Entangled Realities (with Kim Antieau)
Labor Days
Miniatures

Poetry
Animal Life
Fantasy Life
Love Life

The Burning Artist

Mario Milosevic

The Burning Artist
by Mario Milosevic

Copyright © 2014 by Mario Milosevic

Published by Green Snake Publishing

ISBN: 978-1-949644-40-1

Cover image © Philcold | Dreamstime.com

www.greensnakepublishing.com

—*Franz Kafka*

A shy man, in his mid-twenties, leaned on the rail looking down on New York City through the observation windows of the Hindenburg.

"It's getting dark," he said.

"Yes," said the woman beside him. "We will be landing in New Jersey soon."

She did not look at him. He had wanted to speak to her during the last three days but could never find a convenient moment.

"My name is Frederick," he said quietly.

She turned to him, a slight smile on her face. She put out her hand. He touched it lightly. "I am Ann," she said. "May I ask why you have not approached me before this? Our journey is almost over."

He felt his ears turn hot. "Forgive me. Sometimes I lack the courage."

She nodded. "I have noticed you always carry that book with you." She indicated the slim volume in his hand.

"Ah, yes. It is a story about me. When I was very young. A boy. A famous writer wrote it for me."

"Famous?"

"See for yourself."

He handed her the book. The cover bore a drawing of a small boy, and she could see that it was a younger version of the man standing with her now. The title was *Frederick's Zeppelin* by Franz Kafka.

"Franz Kafka," said Ann. "Famous?"

"He wrote about starvation artists and people turning into insects."

She seemed skeptical. "I see."

"Well, perhaps he is not famous now, but he will be. He died very young after being sick for a long time. My father was a Zeppelin pilot years ago. One of the first. He met Mr. Kafka in Berlin and asked him to write a story for me."

"How extraordinary," said Ann.

"Yes, isn't it?"

"What is the story about?"

"A children's tale. A fantasy. But it meant a lot to me when I was growing up. It taught me that things are possible. Many things. For example, back then Zeppelins were experimental craft. And now, here we are on a passenger Zeppelin. Almost routine."

She turned from him and looked down on the lights of buildings passing beneath them. "Yes," she said. "This famous writer. What was his life like?"

"Well, as I say, he was very sick when he wrote this. But he had a friend, a woman, Dora Diamant, who loved him and made his bad times bearable, at least for a while. I met her once when I was just a boy."

How modest these [injured workers] are. They come to us with requests. Instead of storming the company and smashing everything to bits they come with requests.
—Franz Kafka

Dora found a pile of Franz's scribbling by his desk where he had spent the night working on some ridiculous story. She scooped them up and fed them to the flames in the fireplace.

Franz's friend Max had said he would never do as Franz wished, which was to destroy his stories and papers. But Dora had no problems complying with Franz's request. Perhaps if she could destroy all trace of his writing, he would stop his scribbling (Franz's word) and spend more time in the garden, where he could actually do himself some good. Or better yet, more time with her.

She put her hands up to the flames, warming them for a moment, then rose to retrieve the morning mail from the box at the front door. She found a package from Franz's publisher and a letter from her father. He still disapproved of her relationship with Franz. She was fifteen years younger than Franz, they were not married, and Franz was so ill. It was not a proper arrangement in any way, according to her father.

Dora opened the letter and scanned it quickly. She saw that nothing had changed and tossed it into the flames as well.

It was good that her father was still in Poland and she was living here in Berlin with the man she loved. They could have a life together unbound by family expectations.

Dora was prepared to throw the package into the fireplace as well but thought that there might be a check inside. And maybe Franz would enjoy opening it himself. She left it on the table in the small kitchen of their rented house.

She looked out the window. A chilly October morning, but the sun was bright. Franz was bent over the furrows of the backyard garden, scooping up the dirt and pulling weeds. He was not what Dora would call an excellent gardener by any means, but he did seem to enjoy the ritual of it.

She rapped on the window. Franz looked up and smiled. She motioned him inside. It was time to eat breakfast.

He waved. She laughed. He was so small. And so smart. Had he not saved hundreds of lives when he was employed at the Worker's Accident Insurance Company of the Kingdom of Bohemia with his redesigns of mill machinery to make them safer? No one else had done that. No one else had even thought of it.

But that was his life before he became ill. Back in Prague, before she even knew him.

Dora had met Franz only a few months ago and now could not imagine her life without him. It hurt her that he spent so much time at his writing. It seemed to her he was making his health worse by being bent over a desk for hours on end concocting wild stories that *did not make sense*.

She turned to the stove and stirred Franz's scrambled eggs in their pan. The back door swung open and Franz stepped inside the house.

"It's cold," he said.

"You got up so early," said Dora.

"It's the pain, Dora. It makes it hard to sleep."

Dora nodded. "So you get out of bed and scribble?"

Franz went to the sink and began washing his hands. "It gives me something to do. And if I can sell them, it will bring us some extra money. Did you read my pages?"

"I did as you have asked me to do many times, Franz. I burned them."

"Ach! Dora! No. I mean after I *die*. Burn my papers and stories after I have died. Not now."

"And what is the difference? If you don't want them to survive, why not get it over with now?"

Franz dried his hands on a dish towel and sighed. "Dora, Max understands how this works. Why can't you?"

She went to him and embraced him. "Now sit down, and I'll feed you."

Franz sat at the table. "You didn't answer my question," he said.

"Max understands nothing, Franz. You told me yourself he has vowed not to honor your wishes."

Franz picked up the package from his publisher. He turned it over several times, as if deciding whether he should open it or not.

"Max will do as I ask. He is my friend."

"Oh," said Dora. "Max is your *friend*. And what am I, my dear Franz? What am I?"

"Oh, Dora. You know what I mean."

She put a plate in front of him and then scraped

eggs, potatoes, and spinach from the pan onto it. "Here you are, my dear Franz."

"Thank you, Dora." He took a bite of his breakfast. "Did you see the Zeppelin?" he asked.

"No, Franz."

"It passed right over the house. It was so big, Dora. Hard to believe anything that large can be controlled in any way."

"I'm sure they know what they are doing," said Dora. She looked at the package that Franz had placed next to his elbow. "Why don't you open it?" she asked.

"It's just a silly magazine," he said.

"There might be money."

He laughed. "You are so optimistic."

She tilted her head and smiled at him. "Yes, and isn't that why you love me? Isn't that why your parents disapprove of me? I am too optimistic for your own good?"

Franz fell silent. His parents would have preferred that he was not living with Dora. She was almost half his age. So scandalous. In Prague, anyway, where his parents lived. Or Poland. But Berlin was different. Here he found a spirit of freedom. In Berlin you could be anything you wanted to be.

When Franz allowed himself to contemplate his future, he knew it would be a short one. Why not live as he wished, rather than comply with some culturally sanctioned norms?

"Come on, Franz. Open it. Please."

He sighed and looked at Dora's face. He shook his head. "Oh, very well," he said and put his thumb under the flap and tore open the package. A magazine, printed in English, fell out onto the table. It showed a crude cover painting of a lighter than air ship in garish colors. "There, you see," he said.

Dora picked it up and fanned the pages. "Is there a check?"

Franz looked inside the envelope. "Empty."

"Why did your publisher send you this?" She handed the magazine back to Franz.

He opened it to the table of contents and ran his finger down the page. "Here," he said. "They have reprinted one of my stories. 'The Metamorphosis.'" He turned to the indicated page, and his face turned white.

Dora's eyes widened, alarmed. "Franz, what is it?"

"Again with the insect," he said. "Again they must always draw the insect. Why, Dora? I don't want them to draw the insect. We must never *see* the insect."

"Franz, please. Don't get so upset." She took the magazine and looked at the title page of "The Metamorphosis." "It's not such a bad drawing," she said. "Better than the Zeppelin on the cover."

"If I knew my publisher would allow any horrible

magazine to reprint my story, I never would have let them print it in the first place."

"Franz, you are so dramatic. It's a perfectly nice drawing."

Franz held up his hand. "Just put it away, Dora. Please."

"Shall I burn it?" she asked, indicating the fireplace in the front room with a slanting look of her eyes.

Franz laughed. "Dora, you are being silly."

"The envelope, Franz. At least let me burn the envelope. Let me burn something!" She stared at him with very wide eyes. Franz could not help laughing. But his laughter turned to coughing, and he doubled over in pain.

"Franz—"

He held up his hand, and Dora remained motionless. "You should not have been out in the chill, Franz. You know you need the fireplace now. Heat." She went to him and put her hand on his back.

He moved closer to her.

"You should not be with me," he managed to say, hoarsely.

"Shhh," she murmured. "Don't talk now. We will move to Israel as soon as we can."

"Dora, you are young. You should find someone else. Someone who isn't sick like me and dying."

"Don't say that. In the desert you will get better."

He sat up, took several long breaths. "I think I need a nap," he said.

She walked with him to the bedroom, he leaning close to her, she supporting him as best she could. "You know," she said, "there is a reading tonight. That poet you like. What is his name?"

"Dora, no. I couldn't go tonight. Maybe another time."

She tucked him into bed and heard a knock at the front door. "Who could that be?" she said.

Franz rolled over and pulled the covers up to his shoulder. Dora did not want to leave him. She never wanted to be away from him. Another knock on the door. Not impatient, but still there.

She went to the front door and pulled it open. A man stood in front of her.

"Yes?" she said.

"Is this the home of Mr. Franz Kafka? The author?"

She could tell by his accent he was German. Standing beside the man was a young boy, perhaps seven years old. Dora recognized him. He had been at the house a couple of days ago, talking to Franz as he worked in the garden.

"Yes," she said. "What can I do for you?"

She held the door half open, waiting for his answer.

"This is Frederick, my son, and I am Hans." Frederick was staring at his shoes.

"Hello, Frederick," said Dora.

Hans nudged his son. Frederick bent his head even lower. "He's shy," said Hans apologetically.

She nodded.

"Franz was very kind to Frederick the other day."

"He is very fond of children, my Franz. He always listens with both ears."

"Frederick had lost his toy Zeppelin, and Mr. Kafka helped him find it."

Dora nodded again, waiting for this man to explain his visit. She did not let him in. She made no motion to invite either of them into her house.

"I had heard that Mr. Kafka was here in Berlin, but I had no idea— Well. You see, I have admired his stories for many years. I am a Zeppelin pilot. I sense in his stories a spirit that wants to be free. Do you see it, too?"

Dora was growing impatient. Did this man know Franz was sick? Did he know that Mr. Franz Kafka was not able to receive visitors? Should she tell him?

"He has often spoken of trapeze artists with admiration," said Dora. "He admires their freedom."

"Exactly so," said Hans. "I would like to commission him to write a story for me and my Frederick. Frederick is crazy about Zeppelins, you see. I think Mr. Kafka could write a fine story that Frederick would love, and that I could have illustrated as a present for Frederick. I am prepared to pay a handsome sum."

Dora thought of how much money they had. Or rather, of how little. She had been taking in sewing and did some housework for families in the neighborhood. They also had Franz's pension, but that was meager at best. The rent was coming due soon. She did not know where they would find the money. Or how they could possibly get to Israel.

Hans stood with an awkward smile on his face. "I can see I am keeping you, and I do not want to inconvenience either of you. Please accept my card." He handed her a small card with his name and address and phone number. She took it from him. The corner bore a small drawing of a Zeppelin, like the one Franz had seen this morning. But Dora knew Franz did not approve of them.

"They are filled with highly flammable hydrogen gas," he once told her. "One tiny spark and *poof*—an inferno as you would not want to ever witness."

"Thank you," Dora said to Hans. "I will not promise anything, but I will convey to him your request."

Hans touched his hat with this forefinger and tilted his head. "I thank you for your time," he said and then he and Frederick turned around and walked away, down the street.

Dora looked in on Franz. He was breathing rhythmically. No doubt dreaming some wild dream of a story. She closed the door quietly and went back to the kitchen table. The magazine was still there, with the Zeppelin airship on the cover. She put her hand on it and thought of what Franz had said.

Surely he was wrong, she thought. Surely no one would make a ship that could destroy itself so easily.

> *In blessed moments, he was the glowing, shining racing messenger, fully aware of his strength and filled with belief and hope.*
>
> *—Dora Diamant*

Later that morning, when Franz had awakened and gotten over the grogginess of his nap, Dora told him about the visit from Hans. Kafka listened with interest.

"They are dangerous craft, Dora, yes. We would never have approved workers being around them at the insurance company. Much too dangerous. But, you know, there is something intriguing about danger. Remember I told you how much I loved to ride my motorcycle when I was younger? Half the fun was knowing I could be killed in an instant."

"I can never understand such thinking," said Dora.

"Life is dangerous enough without doing things to make it even more threatening."

"Yes, of course, Dora. You are right. It is foolish and ridiculous to put oneself in danger. But many crave it. I think I can understand it."

"So you want to write the story for the boy?"

Franz laughed. "I don't know about that. I have never written anything for children."

"Oh, Franz. How difficult can it be?"

"I have this book I want to finish, Dora. I don't know how much time I have left."

Dora's face flushed. She almost began to cry. "No," she said. "Please, Franz, I have told you. Don't talk that way."

He patted her hand. "I'm sorry Dora. I have been ill for so long, I forget it is still new to you."

She put her other hand on top of his. They did not move for several seconds. Then Franz gently tugged his hand away. She rose and brought the kettle from the stove and filled his cup. He sipped from it.

"This man is German?" he said.

"Yes," said Dora. "But he seemed all right."

"We must be careful in this city. Things can change quickly. It can be very bad for us you know."

"Of course, Franz. I know. I have lived in Berlin for four years already. I know. But not all Germans hate us. He likes your stories."

"Yes," said Franz. "So he says."

"Try a page or two," said Dora. "A children's story doesn't have to be very long. You are a great writer. You can do this."

Franz laughed. He had not laughed for a long time before he met Dora, but around her he was always ready to do so. He was very happy with her.

"I will do it for you," he said, "since you seem so much to want me to."

If there is a transmigration of souls then I am not yet on the bottom rung. My life is a hesitation before birth.

—Franz Kafka

Franz set aside work on "A Hunger Artist," a story he had been contemplating for some time in which a man starves himself as a form of entertainment for an audience.

The image of the thin dying man had come to him soon after he himself had been diagnosed with TB. He felt he understood this hunger artist as a fellow barer of his soul. Did not Franz himself starve for his audience, barely finding enough money to eat, but still writing stories for the public to ponder and think about? In the story, the audience did not understand and threw food at the artist.

Franz was struggling now with the ending, and perhaps it was time for him to set it aside for a few days and try his hand at a children's story.

He took out a fresh sheet of paper and dipped his pen in his inkwell.

He wrote at the top of the page: "Frederick's Zeppelin." He thought for a moment, then began writing. He wrote for an hour or so until he had filled up 5 pages. Then he wrote "THE END" at the bottom of the last page. He read it over once and made a few corrections, then took it to Dora.

"Here it is," he said. "What do you think? I don't know what children like. Do you think Frederick will like it?"

Dora took the pages. Franz looked so small and fragile. "I tried to make it a cheerful story," said Franz.

"That is not your usual way," said Dora.

"No, of course not. But for a child—" He shrugged.

"No need to give a child depressing thoughts?"

Franz smiled. "Yes, yes. Quite so, Dora. Will you read it?"

She appeared to consider this. "After I burn it, or before?"

"Dora, you mock me."

"Yes, I mock you, and yet you smile, Franz."

He left her with the pages and tried to go back to his hunger artist, trapped in a cage, unable to escape his fate or the taunts of his intended audience.

But he found his eyes tracking over the same few words over and over and he was taking none of it in. All he could think about was Dora in the other room, reading his little story for Frederick. How could it take so long to read five pages?

"Dora?" he called. "Are you all right?"

"Franz, please. Let me finish."

He looked out the window. "Don't burn it," he said. "Even if you don't like it. Don't burn it yet."

Then, after a few minutes, he put his head down on his desk and fell asleep again.

> *I have a hellish love of screaming into the ears of a well-prepared, attentive audience.*
>
> *—Franz Kafka*

Dora invited Hans to the house. She cooked him a fine dinner and told him to be patient. Franz would read him the story, but first she wanted Hans to feel at home. Franz sat at the table with them. He looked frail. He was not eating as much as he should. Dora believed with all her soul that if Franz would just rest and eat well he would get better.

"We are thinking of moving to Tel Aviv," she told Hans. "It is our people's home, you see, and the sun would do Franz good. We would open up a restaurant. I am a wonderful cook—so Franz tells me—and it would be so good for us."

Hans was visibly uncomfortable being in their home. "I had no idea you were ill, Mr. Kafka. I feel as though I have imposed upon you by proposing my commission."

Franz lifted his hand, as though to say it was nothing. He was always precisely mannered and polite. Always so considerate. Dora could not understand how critics and some of the public saw Kafka as a depressing man. He was full of life. His stories were just his stories. There was so much more to him than his scribbling.

"Excuse me for not conversing more," said Franz. "I am saving my voice for my reading."

"We were wondering," said Dora as she put food on Hans's plate, "how you can pilot a craft like the Zeppelin. I mean, knowing how dangerous it is."

Franz looked at Dora, surprised by her forwardness.

"Danger?" said Hans.

"The hydrogen," said Dora. "My Franz tells me it

can burn up like that—" She snapped her fingers. The sound was like an exclamation point in the air.

Hans laughed. "Many have warned me of this," he said. "But Zeppelins have flown for many thousands of hours already with no accident."

"It only takes one," said Dora.

He nodded. "Of course. But there are safeguards. One can smoke only in a sealed area. And we take every precaution to insure the gas is also completely sealed. It is always away from the passengers. You know, we Germans understand engineering very well. We know how to make these things as safe as humanly possible."

"I see," said Dora.

They ate in silence. After the meal, Dora served them all coffee in the front room. Hans seemed more comfortable now. He sat on the couch and Dora looked to Franz.

Franz put his cup down and stood up. Dora resisted an urge to go over and help him. This little story may have meant very little to him at first, but now he wanted to make this reading as good as possible. Hans waited politely until Franz drew himself up to his full height. "The story is called 'Frederick's Zeppelin,'" said Franz. "I hope you enjoy it."

Hans's face had reddened slightly. He looked at Dora who smiled back.

"Frederick was a very smart boy and very good, too. His parents loved him and cared for him and made sure he had plenty of food to eat and plenty of toys to play with.

"He was such a good and smart boy that his parents wanted him to have a very nice present. Frederick's father was a Zeppelin pilot and Frederick loved Zeppelins. One day his parents told him that they had gotten him a Zeppelin all for himself.

"Well, Frederick was as happy as he could be, but he knew that Zeppelins were dangerous things. They could burn up because they were filled with hydrogen gas.

"'I would love to have my very own Zeppelin,' said Frederick, 'but I would want to make improvements.'

"'What sort of improvements?' asked his mother.

"'I would fill the Zeppelin with helium instead of hydrogen because helium does not burn.'

"Frederick's mother and father were very impressed with how smart Frederick was. 'That is an excellent idea,' said his father. 'But where are you going to get the helium?'

"Frederick did not know, exactly, but he said he would think about it.

"Then Frederick's parents told him that since he had explained to them the danger of a hydrogen-filled Zeppelin, they had decided that they should not get him his very own full-sized Zeppelin after all, but they would think about getting him a smaller toy Zeppelin.

"Frederick was very sad. He went outside and walked down the street to the house where the man spent many minutes each day working in his garden. Frederick told the man what happened and how sad he was. The man listened and said he was sorry Frederick did not get his Zeppelin, but why didn't he just get some helium?

"'But where can I get helium?' said Frederick.

"'Haven't you ever been to a birthday party? Or a carnival?' asked the man.

"Frederick didn't know what that had to do with it. He left the man to his gardening and returned home. He read many books and talked to many experts. They all said helium was very hard to get. It came from natural gas and Frederick did not know where to get natural gas.

"Then one day Frederick's parents told him they were taking him to the circus. At the circus Frederick had a lot of fun. He watched elephants and clowns. He ate fluffy candy and loved to see the trapeze artists flying through the air. He also saw many children holding strings attached to balloons that tried to float up to the ceiling. They were filled with helium.

"Now Frederick knew exactly what he must do. He would collect helium filled balloons from all his friends and after a while he would have enough balloons to fill a Zeppelin.

"All his friends said they thought that would be a good idea, and they brought over their balloons when they were finished playing with them. Frederick's room was soon filled with balloons, and when he had collected about a million million million of them, he told his parents, who immediately went out and got him the Zeppelin they had promised.

"Frederick was so happy. He became an expert Zeppelin pilot and gave rides to all his friends.

"He even took his Zeppelin to the gardener's house. He offered the gardener and the lady he lived with a ride on the Zeppelin. The gardener thought about it for a long time. Then he and the gardener's friend got on the Zeppelin with Frederick.

"They rose above the city and looked down on all the people who looked so small.

"'Thank you for the ride,' said the gardener.

"'Yes, thank you very much,' said the gardener's friend.

"'Thank you,' said Frederick, 'for helping me figure out where to find helium.'

"After that, Frederick took his Zeppelin all around the world, seeing many new places and meeting many new people. They all loved Frederick and his Zeppelin and they all wanted rides. Frederick was very happy showing off his Zeppelin. He gave rides to anyone who asked, and he was very very happy for a very very long time.

"The End"

Franz sat down as soon as he finished the story. The room was completely silent. Dora turned to Hans.

"Well," she said. "What do you think?"

Franz realized, too late, that what he had done was invite a critic into his house. He had never done anything like this before. The people who read his stories were always distant from him. They had never been face to face with him before. This fact unsettled him. What if Hans did not like the story? Then all this would have been for nothing, as he could not publish this story anywhere else. It was a story for Frederick. About Frederick.

Hans rose and went to Franz and pumped his hand vigorously. "Thank you," he said. "Thank you for this. I think Frederick will adore it. I had no idea that my own son would be in a story written by Mr. Franz Kafka."

Franz nodded very sightly. He was tired, but this felt good. This adoration and gratitude. He was surprised what it did to his soul. How alive it made him feel.

Dora was beaming. The story was a hit, as she knew it would be.

"If I may be so bold," said Hans, "can you tell me how much you pay in rent for this house?"

Dora told him.

"Then here," said Hans, "is enough for three months rent as payment for the story." He handed over a sheaf of notes from his pocket. "Will this be sufficient?"

Dora took the money gratefully. "Yes, of course," she said. "Thank you."

Franz handed Hans the pages. He took them and rolled them into a tube. "I will bring you a copy of the illustrated book when it is finished," he said.

"If it is all right," said Franz, "have the illustrator refrain from drawing the Zeppelin. I think it would serve the story better."

Hans seemed puzzled, but he nodded. "Thank you for your art," he said. "I know Frederick and I will treasure this story always."

And then he was gone. "That was wonderful," said Dora. "Wasn't it marvelous, Franz? Wasn't that just amazing?"

But Franz had fallen asleep. Dora put a blanket over him to keep him warm. She watched him for many minutes, then went to the kitchen to clean up.

No, not a request, just breath, not breath,
just readiness, not readiness, just a thought,
not a thought, just peaceful sleep.
                              —Franz Kafka

A couple of weeks later Dora and Franz were in the front room, Dora sewing and Franz reading the newspaper, where he found a story about a socialist party headed by someone named Hitler. In Munich, he and his men forced their way into a town meeting, brandishing submachine guns. Franz was very troubled by this turn of events. Dora tried to console him.

"Munich is far away," she said.

"Yes, but this madness can spread, Dora."

She had nothing to offer in answer.

Franz's condition had not improved very much. He worked on his stories when he could, but it was difficult for him.

"We have money for a while," she said. "Franz, why not let it go? It takes so much out of you."

How could he tell her he sensed his time was short, and he needed to finish what work he could? Perhaps he could produce something that he would not want to consign to the flames.

What Dora did not tell her Franz was that Hans had offered him a ride in his Zeppelin, as gratitude for the story. She had assured him that Franz was not interested. And yet, she was not so sure at all.

"Did you see the Zeppelin this morning?" said Franz.

"Yes," said Dora. "It is quite amazing, isn't it?"

"You know, Dora, maybe I was wrong about that craft. Maybe it is safe."

"Oh, Franz, you said yourself a terrible accident was practically assured at some time."

"Yes, I said this," said Franz. "And yet. I find myself dreaming of it. Did I tell you? I have dreamed that I have turned into that balloon. Can you imagine?"

Dora laughed. "From reading your stories, Franz, it is little wonder that you would dream such a thing."

"I floated up," said Franz. "You know some critics have taken my little insect story to task. They have said that in 'The Metamorphosis' my poor Gregor can easily fly away. He has wings, but he never uses them. They say it is as though he is too stupid to understand that he can escape his predicament."

"Yes, Franz, and what do you think of this criticism?"

Franz drew a ragged breath. "I wish I had learned to fly when I was younger. When I was healthier. Now—" He held up his hand and rubbed his fingers against his thumb, then spread his hand, as though releasing a bit of air. "I feel as though I am nothing. I feel like I am no longer even here."

"Like your hunger artist?"

"I am so cold, Dora. Why must it be so difficult, now? So hard to live?"

She had no answer for him.

"I think of the burning Zeppelins to come," he said. "What is to become of us, Dora? I fear for the future. There is so much that can go wrong. I have written of broken people and broken societies, but I know next to nothing about it.

"It can all become so much worse."

I hope to sit on a chair in a very distant land one day, and see sugar cane fields from my office window.

—Franz Kafka

A light wind swept over the field, rippling the grass almost playfully. It was perfect weather for a Zeppelin ride. Hans stood at the bottom of the ramp, his hand on a railing. Franz, so thin and quiet, stood behind him.

The ground crew worked around them, preparing the vast ship, looming over them like a second sky. Hans had secured permission for his distinguished passenger. Dora approached Hans.

"You must take care of him," she said. "He is my life. I am letting him go because I think it will be good for him, but if anything happens to him, I will not forgive you. Do you understand?"

Hans tried to smile, but he felt the force of her

words. "I would not board this craft, much less pilot it, if I thought anything would happen to either of us," he said. "You know, in the future, in the very near future, passengers will fly regularly on Zeppelins."

Dora did not look away from his eyes. Hans reached into his jacket and pulled out a large book. On the cover was a portrait of Frederick. Under it the words "Frederick's Zeppelin, by Franz Kafka." "You see," said Hans, "I would not do something that would keep me from my own son."

Dora went to Franz and embraced him.

"Thank you for this," he said.

She had tears on her cheek. He wiped them off. "Don't worry," he said. "It is a small danger at best. None of the crew smokes, you see. It will be all right. Did you know, Dora, that my first published writing was of an air show in Rome?"

"Oh, Franz. What does it matter now? You will be floating above the Earth. Isn't that enough?"

"Like my poor Gregor never did?"

She nodded.

"Don't burn any of my papers."

She laughed. "Yet, you mean."

"Yes. You must wait for the proper time."

He turned and stepped up the ramp and into the narrow corridor that led to a catwalk. Hans walked in front of him toward the front of the gondola slung under the big balloon. An amazing flower of radiating steel work bloomed above him in the vast space enclosed by the Zeppelin's skin.

Now he saw how it would be. He would go with Hans to the control room. He would sit beside Hans and look through the window at the ground. Dora would wave at him and he would wave back. Hans and his crew would ready their craft and then he would rise.

Dora would shrink on the ground to a point, but Franz Kafka would break the bonds of Earth for a short time and float free. He would be part of the sky. He would live as trapeze artists live. He would reach for the stars for a brief, floating, glorious moment.

We need the books that affect us like a disaster, that grieve us deeply, like the death of someone we loved more than ourselves.

—Franz Kafka

"How extraordinary," said Ann. "Your father gave him a ride in the Zeppelin?"

Frederick nodded.

"What happened to Mr. Kafka and Dora?"

"He died the next year. Dora did move to Israel. I think she lives there now."

"And did she burn his papers?"

"I have heard that she did. Many of his last stories have been lost because of it."

"She must have loved him very much to follow his wishes."

Frederick looked down at the darkness beneath them. Lakehurst was somewhere in that murk. "Love, perhaps," he said. "But wouldn't it have been better to try to keep his name alive in the world? Wouldn't that have been more of an act of love?"

"People love in different ways."

"Yes, of course. His friend, you know, Max Brod, has taken many of Kafka's stories and is publishing them."

"There, you see?" said Ann. "Another form of love."

Frederick tilted his head and smiled. "As you say."

Ann still held the book in her hands. "This is his only children's story?" She ran her palm over the cover.

"Yes."

"And your father made a copy for him?"

"Yes, of course. Though I'm sure Dora burned it."

Ann seemed to consider this for a time. "May I read it?"

He consented, and she went to one of the tables and

ordered a drink and opened the cover. He felt a peculiar thrill, watching her read his story.

The Hindenburg glided toward the docking tower. Frederick watched as ropes dropped down and the ground crew scurried about to secure them. Many spectators from around the area had come to watch this extraordinary craft come to rest. Frederick looked down on the field, lit by landing lights.

And felt a tremor.

Then a thundering.

Heat rising, the ship falling.

Flames bloomed everywhere, walls of them. Frederick heard terrified screams.

The cabin tipped backwards. Metal screeched. Panicked, he looked towards Ann, who had fallen out of her chair and was sliding along the floor. He reached for her, but she was not close enough. She kept sliding and crashed into the far wall.

Frederick's hand was still wrapped around the railing and he held on with all his might.

The book, Franz Kafka's children's book, followed Ann along the floor. The flames entered the cabin now. The heat was too much. The walls disintegrated around him, and Frederick fell through the floor.

He seemed to fly in the darkness. He thought only of the book. The wonderful little story of the little boy, now consigned to flames. Burning in the wreckage of this ship.

The ground, terrifying in the darkness, rose to meet him and smashed him on contact. He groaned in the darkness. Rescuers took him away.

Later he would recover from his broken bones and his burned skin. He would find Ann, and they would embrace as though they had been lovers.

They had survived the wreck of the great Hindenburg.

But Franz Kafka's little story of the little boy who took helium from balloons, that little story, as its creator had always wished, was nothing now but memory and ash.

He wanted to burn everything he had written in order to free his soul. I respected his wish.

—Dora Diamant

Mario Milosevic's books include *The Coma Mono-logues, Animal Life, Claypot Dreamstance, The Last Giant, Terrastina and Mazolli*, and many others. His honors include nominations for the Puschcart Prize and the Rhysling Award.

9 781949 644401